DRAGONBREATH
NIGHTMARE
OF THE IGUANA

DRAGONBREATH

NIGHTMARE OF THE IGUANA

BY

URSULA VERNON

DIAL BOOKS
an imprint of Penguin Group (USA) Inc.

For Mz. Faunce

DIAL BOOKS
An imprint of Penguin Group (USA) Inc.
Published by The Penguin Group • Penguin Group (USA) Inc., 375 Hudson Street, New York, NY 10014, U.S.A. • Penguin Group (Canada), 90 Eglinton Avenue East, Suite 700, Toronto, Ontario, Canada M4P 2Y3 (a division of Pearson Penguin Canada Inc.) • Penguin Books Ltd, 80 Strand, London WC2R 0RL, England • Penguin Ireland, 25 St. Stephen's Green, Dublin 2, Ireland (a division of Penguin Books Ltd) • Penguin Group (Australia), 707 Collins Street, Melbourne, Victoria 3008, Australia (a division of Pearson Australia Group Pty Ltd) • Penguin Books India Pvt Ltd, 11 Community Centre, Panchsheel Park, New Delhi - 110 017, India • Penguin Group (NZ), 67 Apollo Drive, Rosedale, Auckland 0632, New Zealand (a division of Pearson New Zealand Ltd) • Penguin Books, Rosebank Office Park, 181 Jan Smuts Avenue, Parktown North 2193, South Africa • Penguin China, B7 Jaiming Center, 27 East Third Ring Road North, Chaoyang District, Beijing 100020, China • Penguin Books Ltd, Registered Offices: 80 Strand, London WC2R 0RL, England

Designed by Jennifer Kelly
Text set in Stempel Schneidler
Printed in the U.S.A.

10 9 8 7 6 5 4 3 2

Library of Congress Cataloging-in-Publication Data
Vernon, Ursula.
Nightmare of the iguana / by Ursula Vernon. p. cm. — (Dragonbreath ; 8)
Summary: Wendell the iguana's dreams are all nightmares and a Dream Wasp wants him as a host for its eggs—so, with Great-Grandfather Dragonbreath's help, Danny the dragon and Suki the salamander enter Wendell's dreams to try and defeat the wasp.
ISBN 978-0-8037-3846-1 (hardcover)
1. Nightmares—Juvenile fiction. 2. Iguanas—Juvenile fiction. 3. Dragons—Juvenile fiction. 4. Salamanders—Juvenile fiction. 5. Wasps—Juvenile fiction. 6. Best friends—Juvenile fiction. [1. Adventure and adventurers—Fiction. 2. Nightmares—Fiction. 3. Iguanas—Fiction. 4. Dragons—Fiction. 5. Salamanders—Fiction. 6. Wasps—Fiction. 7. Best friends—Fiction. 8. Friendship—Fiction.] I. Title. II. Series: Vernon, Ursula. Dragonbreath ; 8.
PZ7.V5985Nig 2013
813.6—dc23 2012010861

THEY WERE AFTER HIM.

THE MONSTERS WERE GOING TO FIND HIM ANY MINUTE NOW.

THERE WERE DIFFERENT KINDS, AND THEY CARRIED PAPERS IN THEIR LONG CLAWS.

IT WAS THE QUIZ HE HADN'T STUDIED FOR!

WHAT IS THE CAPITAL OF URUGUAY?
WHAT YEAR WAS NAPOLEON DEFEATED AT WATERLOO?
DESCRIBE IN YOUR OWN WORDS THE ROLE OF THE EAST INDIA TEA COMPANY IN THE CONFLICT BETWEEN . . .

IF A LIGHTBULB FACTORY MAKES TEN LIGHTS AN HOUR AND ANOTHER FACTORY MAKES SIX LIGHTS AN HOUR, HOW MANY LIGHTS WILL BE MADE AFTER . . .
SHOW YOUR WORK!

WHAT IS THE ANSWER?
WELL?
TELL ME THE ANSWER!
USE A #2 PENCIL!
WHAT IS IT?

DARK DREAMS

Wendell the iguana was having problems.

He had problems normally, mostly related to his mother's obsession with health food. After the past week, though, bran waffles and beet casserole held little terror for him. Not even the threat of Tofu Surprise* for the weekend could trouble him.

Wendell was having nightmares.

*The surprise is *even more tofu!*

It wasn't just one nightmare, either. It was *all* of them.

Monsters chased him, carrying quizzes he hadn't studied for, making him late for class, while his teeth fell out, and when he got to the class that he hadn't been to all semester, it was being taught by the goldfish he had forgotten to feed for the last ten years. And he wasn't wearing any clothes.

Then he generally fell off a cliff.

Wendell knew that you were always supposed to wake up before you landed, but he didn't. He didn't die, either. Anybody who said you died in real life if you died in a dream was wrong. Sometimes he just hit the ground and then got up again and wandered around—for some reason, he always landed in the desert—and then the whole thing would start up again.

He didn't wake up feeling rested. He woke up feeling like he'd been driven over by a steamroller, and when he dragged himself down to breakfast, his mother would make him drink a vile concoction made of brewer's yeast and macrobiotic kelp proteins, because "you look a little off, honey."

He didn't tell his mom about the nightmares. She'd take him to see a therapist.

But he had to do something. Thursday he'd gotten an A minus on a test.

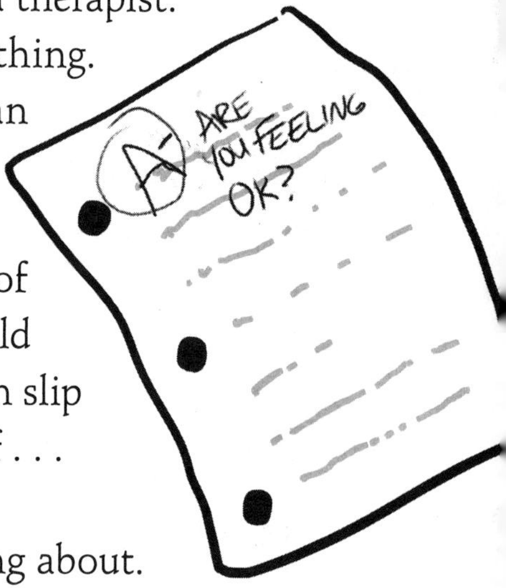

An A *minus.*

After another week of nightmares, what would happen? Might he even slip into the dark realms of . . . *B plus?*

It didn't bear thinking about.

And Danny Dragonbreath, his very best friend in the world, would listen to him, but he might not understand. Danny thought a B plus was a gift from heaven. Danny would be sympathetic about the nightmares, but he was just a kid, like Wendell, and he might not know what to do.

He needed to talk to an adult. Somebody who knew things. Somebody who might be able to help.

GREAT-GRANDFATHER DRAGONBREATH? HI. IT'S ME, WANDA . . .

CANDY CURE

"I can't believe you called my grandfather," said Danny, draping himself over the back of the bus seat. "You hate talking to my grandfather! He always gets your name wrong."

"I thought he might be able to help," said Wendell, clutching his tail tightly.

Danny considered. This was not unreasonable. Great-Granddad Dragonbreath was a repository of all kinds of knowledge. He could read your past lives and he knew stuff about fairies and ninjas and all kinds of cool stuff.

He was also crotchety and mostly deaf, couldn't keep any of his grandkids' names straight, and was convinced that fairies were stealing his spoons. Still, he was a good dragon to have at your back. "Well?"

"Well what?"

"Maybe." Wendell frowned. "Can you spend the night tonight? He told me what to look for, but I can't do it myself. You have to watch and see what happens while I sleep."

"Sure!" said Danny. He couldn't think of anything more boring than watching somebody sleep, but maybe there would be monsters. Monsters would be *awesome.*

Christiana Vanderpool, who was definitely Wendell's friend and more or less Danny's, got on the bus at the next stop and plopped down on the seat next to the iguana. "Hey."

"Hey."

"Hey."

"There was a show on last night about worms that live in deep-sea volcanic vents," said Christiana. "Did you see it?"

"I saw some of it," said Wendell. He'd fallen asleep halfway through, but fortunately a really loud commercial had woken him up before the monsters could corner him and begin asking him about square roots. "It was cool, I guess."

"There were tube worms as big as your arm! They could only live in water that was super-heated from volcanoes, so they had to survive in a zone like six inches wide around the vent! And they were bright red and hundreds of years old!"

Danny was willing to admit that this sounded both cool *and* amazing. Super-heated volcano worms! He wondered if you could keep one in a goldfish bowl with a space heater under it.

"It was amazing, then," said Wendell dutifully.

Christiana took a closer look at him. "You don't look so good."

"I haven't been sleeping well."

Christiana frowned. "Have you tried melatonin? The claims about it are drastically overinflated, but there seems to be solid experimental evidence that it helps you get to sleep."

Wendell sighed. Sleep wasn't the problem. He was so tired that he had started to fall asleep right after dinner. It was just that he spent his sleeping time running away from nightmares, and so he wasn't getting any *rest.*

"He's having nightmares," said Danny helpfully, dangling over the back of the seat some more.

Christiana shrugged. "Well, that's different. There's all sorts of stuff you can try with autohypnosis and whatnot, but if any of them work, it's probably luck and the placebo effect."

THE WHAT EFFECT?

PLACEBO.
IT'S WHERE SOMETHING WORKS BECAUSE YOU BELIEVE IT DOES. LIKE IF YOU HAVE A HEADACHE AND I GIVE YOU A PILL, YOUR HEADACHE GOES AWAY, EVEN IF THE PILL IS AN M&M.

. . . M&M'S CURE HEADACHES?

Christiana had been around Danny quite a bit by now, and so did not sigh or scream or attempt to pitch him out the bus window, no matter how much she might want to. "No," she said. "It works because you believe it should work, not because it really does anything. It's all in your head."

"Ohhhhh," said Danny, understanding. There were lots of things that were all in people's heads. Not his, of course. Wendell, though . . . Wendell had a lot of stuff that was all in his head.

Nerd stuff, mostly. The history of Western Civilization, including dates, and the value of pi worked out to forty places, and most of the periodic table.

And nightmares, apparently.

"Don't worry, dude," said Danny as the bus pulled into the parking lot with a hiss of air brakes. "I'll come over tonight and we'll get this all sorted out."

ARE YOU ASLEEP NOW?

“Okay,” said Wendell, consulting his notes. “He said there are three possibilities.”

“Lay ’em on me,” said Danny. He had just had a dinner so healthy that he had nearly expired on the spot. This would have put him in a bad mood, except that Danny was an expert at staying at Wendell’s house and had brought a backpack full of snacks and some slightly squashed cupcakes, so their *second* dinner had been really good. He was still picking bits of frosting out of his teeth.

THE FIRST ONE'S A NIGHT MARE. IT'S LIKE A BIG HORSE THAT RIDES INTO YOUR DREAMS AT NIGHT.

NEAT!
THE NEXT ONE IS SANDMEN. THEY COME AND FEED OFF YOUR DREAMS. YOU'LL FIND SAND IN THE BED, THOUGH, AND I HAVEN'T SEEN ANY, BUT IT MIGHT JUST BE FADING AWAY TOO QUICKLY...

THE LAST ONE'S A *DREAM WASP.* IT CAN LOOK LIKE ALMOST ANYTHING, BUT IT FEELS LIKE SOMEBODY'S SITTING ON YOUR CHEST AND CRUSHING YOU. NOBODY ELSE CAN SEE IT, THOUGH.

Danny was forced to admit that this was more cool in theory than in practice. Still, he was a bit disappointed they'd attached to Wendell instead of to him. He'd totally handle freaky dream monsters better than the iguana. Wendell could barely handle *breakfast*.

Still, if Wendell was in trouble, Danny wasn't going to let him go it alone. "So what am I looking for?"

Wendell checked his notes again. "If it's a Night Mare, there will be glowing hoofprints. And if it's Sandmen, you'll see sand piling up right in the bed. The Dream Wasp . . . well, he said you'd probably smell something funny."

"What, like dream farts?"

Wendell rolled his eyes. "Your great-granddad didn't say. He just said that you'd know it if you smelled it. And it's possible there's more than one thing. Apparently Night Mares are scavengers, like jackals, and super-common, and they might show up if some other dream predator had already . . . er . . . latched on . . . to pick up the leftovers . . ."

Wendell was looking a little green. Danny patted his shoulder. "It'll be fine. We'll figure it out. We kept you from turning into a were–hot dog, didn't we?"

It turned out that falling asleep with somebody watching was not easy.

At all.

ARE YOU ASLEEP?
NOT YET.
HOW 'BOUT NOW?
NO.
HOW 'BOUT—
NOT HELPING!

Wendell lay in bed and tried not to look at the clock. He had to get up at seven to watch his favorite cartoon, and it was ten thirty now, so if he went to sleep right this minute, he'd get eight and a half hours of sleep. No, now it was ten thirty-one, so he'd get eight hours and twenty-nine minutes. Wait, now it was ten thirty-two, so that was eight hours and twenty-eight minutes . . .

It occurred to him that this was not productive. He shut his eyes and rolled over so that he wouldn't be tempted to peek.

It was even harder to sleep knowing that Danny was lurking somewhere at the foot of the bed, watching him. He could feel the dragon staring at him. He put a pillow over his head.

Danny wasn't having an easy time either. It turned out that watching someone try to fall asleep was boring.

Like, *really* boring.

Nothing was happening at all, and if you tried to hurry it up, it actually took longer.

Danny eventually pulled out a comic book and started to read. He was yawning himself, and had to pinch his own tail repeatedly to stay awake. When the comic book had gone blurry and dull for the third time, he set it down and looked over at Wendell.

The iguana was dead to the world. Mr. Higgins the stuffed bunny was tucked under his arm. As Danny watched, Wendell started to snore.

It was a commanding snore for such a small lizard. It started with a sort of "Sng-sng-*snggk* . . ." and grew to a full-throated "Hgrrrrrnnnnk!" Danny was grudgingly impressed.

Nothing else happened.

Danny waited, much more awake now—surely it was about to get good! There would be monsters!—but still nothing happened.

Wendell rolled over, which damped the snoring for about five seconds, and then he started up again. Danny wasn't sure how he managed to sleep through this when he spent the night.*

Nothing continued to happen.

Just when Danny was about to give up and go to sleep himself, Wendell's snores changed.

"Hggnnk . . . hnn . . . kk . . . no . . . stop . . . go *away* . . ."

"Wendell?" asked Danny, worried.

The iguana moaned in his sleep.

This was not cool. Wendell sounded really miserable.

And then the nightmares came.

*Danny's parents could have testified that once Danny fell asleep, nothing short of bombs going off would wake him up again.

WHAT'S THE BUZZ?

For Danny, sitting next to Wendell's bed, the first sign was hoofprints. Strange *glowing* hoofprints.

They started up near the ceiling and walked down the wall over the head of Wendell's bed. Danny fell backward, startled. You just didn't expect to see hoofprints coming down the wall at you!

"Dude," he said. "Spider-horse!"

Each hoofprint was the size of a

saucer, and lasted for a few seconds before it faded away.

He tried to remember what Wendell had said. Hoofprints meant a Night Mare. So there was a big evil horse invading Wendell's dreams. That was . . . well . . . not *cool,* exactly, but certainly interesting.

The hoofprints reached the head of the bed. It looked like there might be more than one of them, and they'd all made a beeline for Wendell.

Still, now that they knew what it was, Danny could wake Wendell up. The iguana was moaning louder now, and starting to thrash around in the blankets. Mr. Higgins had slipped unnoticed to the floor.

Danny sat up. He'd grab Wendell's shoulder and shake him, that ought to work. And if that didn't, there was still a glass of water on the nightstand; he could just dump it over the iguana's head.

Come to think of it, that would be a lot more fun to begin with . . .

He was reaching for the glass of water when the smell hit him.

The smell wasn't bad, exactly, but it was really strong. It smelled like lemon floor cleaner, only with some weird spices thrown in. Danny felt like he'd shoved a cough drop up his nose.

The glowing hoofprints, which had stopped over the head of Wendell's bed, suddenly began to move again. Danny couldn't really tell, given that the Night Mares were invisible and all, but he'd swear that they'd begun milling about uncertainly on the wall over the bed.

The cough-drop smell got even stronger. Danny's eyes started to water, and he scrubbed at his nose with the back of his hand.

Suddenly the hoofprints turned around and fled upward, toward the ceiling. They stopped at the top of the wall, as if the owners of the hooves had vanished through the roof.

Had something scared them away?

The smell was so thick that Danny could feel it on his tongue and the back of his throat. He was amazed that Wendell's mom couldn't smell it down the hall.

A vibration seemed to fill the air, then a strange whining note. It sounded like distant power tools, as if somebody was using a chain saw or a weed whacker outside. Danny looked around wildly for the source, but he couldn't find anything. Nobody was going to use a chain saw in the middle of the night, not in this neighborhood.

The vibration got louder. Danny could feel it through the soles of his feet. Mr. Fins, Wendell's geriatric goldfish, swam agitated circles in his bowl.

Danny was sure that Wendell's mom was going to burst in the door at any moment, and that would be bad. I mean, not that he was doing anything *wrong,* exactly, but . . . well, in Danny's experience, there were very few situations that were improved by having Wendell's mother around.

The dragon was on his feet and looking around wildly when he realized what the sound was.

It was *buzzing.*

"Dream Wasp!" said Danny. "Of course—the smell—" His great-granddad hadn't mentioned buzzing, but what else could it be? It sounded as if an entire hive of yellow jackets had moved into the walls of the room, possibly carrying weed whackers.

"Noooooo . . ." moaned Wendell.

Danny was sure of one thing. This had gone far enough. The Night Mares had been kinda cool, but there was nothing cool about this buzzing. It was a nasty, angry, whiny noise. No good was going to come of a noise like this.

He grabbed Wendell's shoulder and shook it. "Wendell! Wendell, get up!"

"The square root . . ." Wendell moaned into his pillow. "I have to find the square root . . ."

"Forget the square root, Wendell! We have problems!"

The buzzing hadn't gotten louder, but it was *concentrating* in a way Danny didn't like at all. Now it sounded like a whole hive of hypothetical yellow jackets, who were directly behind Wendell's headboard.

The stench of lemon cough drop was so strong it was making Danny's nose run. He scraped his shirt sleeve across his snout and it left a wet stain.

"Wendell!" Danny grabbed the glass of water. "Get up, NOW!"

He dumped the glass over the iguana's head.

Wendell flailed around and sat up in bed. The buzzing had stopped as soon as he had opened his eyes, and Danny was pretty relieved about that. It had not been a nice sound. It had been about as far from nice as a sound could get.

"Oh, maaaaan . . ." Wendell looked down at himself. He was dripping wet and the sheets were soaked. It looked like he'd wet the bed, even if it was just a glass of water. "I'm gonna have to get this into the dryer or Mom's gonna kill me . . ."

"We've got bigger problems," said Danny grimly. "You've got Night Mares, and something a lot worse."

MAGICAL, MYTHICAL JAPAN

Saturday morning came bright and early. Danny hadn't slept well.

Every time Wendell fell asleep again, the dragon lay there and waited for that awful buzzing to start up. By the time morning came around, he needed a nap very badly.

Breakfast didn't help. Danny and Wendell had been friends long enough that Wendell no longer felt obligated to apologize for what his mom served for breakfast. Fortunately Wendell's mom was too busy to make bran waffles that day, and the granola was okay if you picked out the woody bits.

"Are you sure you don't want some brewer's yeast, honey?" she asked Wendell, bustling around the kitchen.

"I'm fine, Mom," said Wendell.

"Okay. I'm off to my drum circle. You boys have fun, and put your dishes in the sink when you're done."

"What's a drum circle?" Danny asked when Wendell's mom had left.

"A bunch of people get together and chant and bang on drums."

An hour of their favorite cartoons and some contraband cupcakes from Danny's backpack revived them somewhat. "Anyway," said Danny as they left the house, "we can sleep on the bus."

"What bus?" asked Wendell.

"The bus to Great-Granddad's house, of course."

Wendell sighed. Talking to Great-Grandfather Dragonbreath on the phone was bad enough. In person, he tended to be rather . . . overwhelming.

There was also the slight problem that he lived in mythical Japan, which was not easily accessible from the real world as Wendell knew it, except by bus and only if Danny was involved. Buses just plain worked differently when Danny was riding on them.

Still, he seemed to be the only grown-up who had any idea what might be tormenting Wendell. According to Danny, there were both Night Mares and Dream Wasps, and you probably couldn't get rid of those with melatonin and brewer's yeast.

The iguana fell asleep on the bus. Danny sighed. It meant that he'd have to stay awake—you could completely miss some of the more mythological bus stops if you weren't watching for them—but Wendell probably needed the sleep. There wasn't any weird buzzing, anyhow, so maybe the monsters had a hard time getting to you if you were in a moving vehicle.

That was a hopeful thought, but it seemed unlikely that Wendell's mom would be willing to drive Wendell around all night so that he could get a decent night's sleep in the back of the car.

He must have dozed a bit, though, because it seemed like no time at all until the bus driver announced "Headquarters, Celestial Bureaucracy" at the edge of a large office park, and that meant the next stop was mythical Japan and Great-Granddad's house.

He thumped Wendell. Wendell went "Hrrazzzh!" and sat up.

“Mythical Japan!” bawled the bus driver, and Danny yanked the cord to signal a stop. The bus halted in a thick forest of bamboo, and the dragon and iguana got off into the snow.

“Why is it always snowy here?” asked Wendell, stomping through the light blanket of white. “It’s not even winter back home.”

"Ask Great-Granddad," said Danny. "I think it's something to do with magic."

A DREAMY REUNION

Great-Grandfather Dragonbreath's house looked pretty much like it had the last time—a tall building with a layered roof and big statues out in front. The front walk had been shoveled recently. Danny and Wendell trudged up the steps and Danny banged on the door.

"Great-Granddad! It's us!"

"Come in! It's open!"

Great-Grandfather Dragonbreath was an ancient dragon with long whiskers and antlers rather like a deer. He spent most of his time in an equally ancient recliner that appeared to have come from some Paleolithic dawn of time. It was lumpy and dusty and the footrest hung at a strange angle. The old dragon's tendency to stuff his hoard into the cushions didn't help.

He got up out of the recliner now, however. "Danny! Oh, and . . ." He peered over his glasses. ". . . Wanda. Yes."

"Why is it always snowy here, Mr. Dragonbreath?" asked Wendell.

"Eh? Doughy-ear? Kind of mushroom, isn't it? Grows on old tree trunks or something?"

"Snowy!" yelled Wendell. Danny's great-granddad was getting deafer all the time. "Why is it *snowy here*?"

"Mythopoetic influences!" roared Great-Grandfather Dragonbreath. "Vile things! Affect the weather. It's always foggy and snowy. I had to put in a greenhouse and a space heater just to grow decent tomatoes."

"The bamboo seems to grow okay . . ." said Wendell, waving toward the forest.

"Bamboo grows through anything," said Great-Grandfather Dragonbreath grimly. "Mark my words, Wanda. You could grow that stuff in a mineshaft a mile underground and water it with the tears of donkeys and it'd get twenty feet tall and need pruning. Now, you boys probably want some tea, and if you don't, I do, so come on."

"Do donkeys cry a lot?" asked Wendell, following Danny and his ancient relative into the kitchen. "I've never seen one crying . . ."

"In less civilized eras, they used to tie prisoners down over bamboo thickets," said Great-Grandfather Dragonbreath absently. Crockery rattled as he dug for teacups. "Stuff'd grow right through you given half a chance. Awful way to go."

Danny normally would have had a lot to say about death-by-bamboo-thicket, but his attention had been seized by something else entirely.

Something wearing a black dress, sitting at the kitchen table, reading a book.

She looked up.

"Danny? Wendell?"

"Suki?"

The salamander jumped out of her chair and ran over to hug them both. Danny endured this stoically, and Wendell looked like he actually enjoyed it, but he seemed to have a hard time meeting Suki's eyes.

"So, um," said Wendell, staring at his feet. "I, uh."

"I missed you!" said Suki. "Errr . . . that is . . . uh . . . both of you."

"Um, me too," said Wendell. "Uh—not that we were both—I mean, I didn't miss Danny—"

Danny could only take so much awkward nerd courtship. "What are you doing here?" he asked. Suki had been an exchange student at his school last year, but she'd eventually gone back to Japan, and Danny hadn't expected to see her again.

"Your granddad got me a bus pass," Suki said. "He's teaching me meditative techniques. To help with being a ninja in a past life."

Danny was privately unsure how much help

you really needed with being a reincarnated ninja. Suki had been the notorious assassin Leaping Sword in a past life, which had caused some trouble with a troop of ninja frogs who wanted to make her their queen. Danny and Wendell had helped her sort it out, with the aid of Great-Grandfather Dragonbreath and a group of samurai geckos.

As far as Danny was concerned, being a reincarnated ninja was awesome, and Suki had never seemed to appreciate it nearly enough.

Wendell was equally skeptical. "Really? You want to learn more about being a ninja?"

Danny snickered.

"She's at this stage where she thinks that being scared of things makes you interesting," grumbled Suki. "So she's all, 'Oh no, I'm really scared of thunder!' 'Oh no, I'm really scared of ghosts!' 'Oh no, I'm scared of waterslides!'"

Suki grinned. "It wouldn't work. She just wants to tell you about some horrible traumatic thing that almost nearly happened to her. If nobody's watching, she's totally normal. She just wants attention." The salamander shrugged. "Yesterday she decided she was scared of forks. It's just easier to come hide out here than figure out what the phobia of the day is going to be."

It occurred to Danny that being an only child, while it had its drawbacks, also had a lot going for it.

"Suki also helps weed the tomatoes," said Great-Grandfather Dragonbreath, plonking down the teacups. "You'd think the mythopoetic influences could keep out the weeds, but nooooo . . ." He slid a cup toward Wendell. "Here, Wanda, you look like something that's been living under the refrigerator for a week. Have some tea."

Wendell resigned himself to his jasmine-scented fate.

"So." Great-Grandfather Dragonbreath folded his claws around his teacup and leaned forward. "Tell me what happened."

Danny frowned. "Well . . . once Wendell fell asleep—which took *ages*—"

"Did not," muttered Wendell.

"—first there were these glowing hoofprints coming down the wall."

"Night Mares," said Great-Grandfather Dragonbreath with satisfaction. "Knew it." He slurped tea loudly from his cup. "Well, they're not a big deal. They're attracted to bad dreams, but they don't do any real harm."

"But that wasn't all!" said Danny. "There were the hoofprints first, but then there was this *smell*—"

Great-Grandfather Dragonbreath's head snapped up. "A smell? What kind of smell, boy?"

"Lemony," said Danny. "Like floor cleaner or cough drops or something."

The elder Dragonbreath's face looked like *he'd* swallowed a lemon.

"And then the hoofprints ran away, and there was this buzzing . . ."

"NRRRGHGHHK!" Great-Grandfather Dragonbreath slurped tea wrong and sprayed it out across the kitchen. Suki jumped up and began to pound him on the back.

"Oh god," said Wendell. "It's bad, isn't it? I'm going to die. Things are going to eat my brain. It's bad."

"It's not good, Wanda," said Great-Grandfather Dragonbreath. "If Danny could actually hear buzzing, then that means that the Dream Wasp is a lot more . . . um . . . *present* . . . than it normally is. It's trying to actually get into your head, instead of just siphoning the nightmares off the top."

"Why would it want into *Wendell's* head?" asked Danny, feeling rather jealous. "Does it need somebody to do its homework?"

"I suspect that it's looking for a place to lay its eggs," said Great-Grandfather Dragonbreath. "And if it lays them in Wanda's dreams, he'll go mad and never wake up again."

For a long moment, the only sound in the kitchen was the rattle of teacups, and then Wendell let out a squeak and fainted dead away.

IN SEARCH OF BAKU

"It's not as bad as all that," said Great-Grandfather Dragonbreath, when they'd brought Wendell around. The iguana was sitting up, looking woozy. "I didn't say it was hopeless. Did I say it was hopeless, Suki?"

"No, Dragonbreath-sama."

"That's right. Don't make assumptions. You young people today, always assuming things." He poked Wendell in the chest with a claw.

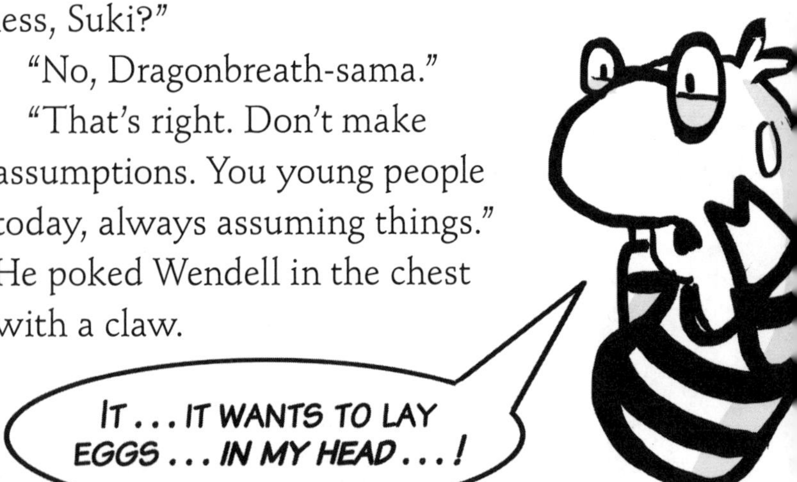

IT . . . IT WANTS TO LAY EGGS . . . *IN MY HEAD* . . . !

“Yes, well, these things happen.” The elder dragon folded his arms inside the sleeves of his robe. “Fortunately not very often, but there are plenty of options. What you need is a baku.”

“What’s a baku?” asked Danny. “Is it like a super-magic sword of Dream Wasp slaying? ’Cause I could totally use one and drop on it from above and go ‘Snicker-Snack!’ and whack its head off—”

“There will be no whacking heads off!” said Great-Grandfather Dragonbreath. “This requires delicacy, not brute force. Start swinging swords around inside Wanda’s head and you’ll give him all kinds of problems! And a baku’s not a what, it’s a who.”

“Well then, *who* is it?”

“A dream-eater,” said Suki, while Great-Grandfather Dragonbreath rinsed out the teapot and started another cup brewing. “They eat nightmares. They’re nice.”

“Well, where do we get one?” asked Danny. He

was a little disappointed that it was not a magic sword, but a dream-eater did sound interesting.

"Oh, that's the easy part. Suki, take them to the baku's pool, will you? I need to think for a bit."

"Sure!" Suki slid off the chair. "Are you going to be okay, sir?"

"Fine, fine . . ." He waved a hand distractedly. "Go bring back a baku, and we'll see what we can do."

"Eggs . . ." said Wendell, staring into his teacup. "In . . . my . . . *head.*"

"Aw, c'mon." Danny grabbed Wendell's arm and hauled him upright. "You'll be fine. We'll go find one of these baku and it'll put you right as rain."

"He's absolutely right, Wanda," said Great-Grandfather Dragonbreath. "You've got the least dangerous job."

Wendell relaxed a little.

"Danny and Suki are going to have to go into your dreams to help the baku find the Wasp, and there's a much better chance they'll be horribly lost forever."

"Awesome!" said Danny.

"What if she gets hurt?" asked Wendell worriedly. "I mean—um—if *they* get hurt?"

"Smooth," muttered Danny. Wendell kicked him under the table.

Suki blushed and stared at the tabletop. "You guys helped me with the ninjas. I mean, it's the least I can do."

"The baku only live about half a mile away," said Suki, shrugging into her jacket. "They like the hot springs. If we're lucky, we can find one that will be willing to help us."

"What if we're not lucky?" asked Wendell.

"Well . . . I suppose we could hit one over the head and stuff it in a sack, but it'd be awfully rude . . ."

Danny grinned. He remembered why he liked Suki.

"I don't know if I want you two going into my dreams," said Wendell, walking down the path with his tail dragging. "I mean, you're my friends and all, but . . . what if there's . . . y'know . . . I mean, it's kinda personal in there . . ."

"I already know about Mr. Higgins," said Danny. "What more could you possibly—"

Wendell kicked him in the shins. Danny hopped on one foot, grinning.

"Mr. Who?" asked Suki.

"Nothing!" said Wendell, giving Danny a Look.

"Aw, it'll be fine," said Danny. "We'll be so busy looking for the Wasp, we won't have time to explore any of your weird fantasies about long division."

Danny wondered what a dream-eater would look like. It'd have fangs, right? You probably needed fangs. Dreams could be scary. And claws. Definitely claws. Big ones like eagles, to grab the wily dream and pin it down. Maybe it would have a giant beak instead of fangs . . .

The reality, as it turned out, was somewhat different.

"So, we're here," said Suki as the bamboo opened up into a clearing.

The clearing was full of rocks, and the rocks were full of pools of water, and the pools of water were full of . . . creatures.

The baku were smaller than Danny, and they had neither fangs nor beaks nor talons. They did have stubby little tusks on their very long snouts, but that was as far as it went. They were white with blue manes, and they all looked about two-thirds asleep.

"They look like *tapirs,*" said Wendell. "Um . . . short little tapirs?"

"I think they're related," said Suki. "The words are almost the same in Japanese. Anyway, these are baku. They eat dreams."

Steam rose from the pools. The little tapir-creatures were basking in the hot water. Danny could hear distant squeaks and murmurs as they bathed.

WHOA.

Several baku had noticed them. A row of long snouts poked over the edge of the nearest pool.

Suki nudged Wendell. "Go up and bow. Introduce yourself."

Wendell took several steps forward. "Er. Um. I'm Wanda. I mean Wendell. Um." He bowed jerkily.

The baku exchanged looks with one another.

"Uh. Yes. I'm having . . . um. A problem."

"He's really a wreck," whispered Suki.

"Yeah," Danny whispered back, "normally he's great at this sort of thing. Must be the lack of sleep."

"Dreams. It's the dreams. I'm having them. Um. They're not good. Bad. Very bad. Yes."

A couple of the baku turned away and went back to soaking in the hot water.

Danny decided to take matters into his own hands. He stepped up next to Wendell and bowed.

"My buddy Wendell here has a real problem. There's a Dream Wasp trying to lay eggs in his head!"

A murmur ran through the assembled baku. It wasn't exactly words. Suddenly there were a lot more snouts aimed at poor Wendell, and they looked only half asleep instead of two-thirds.

"So, uh, yeah." Danny looked across the sea of snouts. "We were hoping one of you'd be able to help. My great-granddad sent us."

The baku all looked at Wendell. Wendell gulped.

There was a splash, and one of the larger baku got out of the water. It was nearly the size of Wendell, and it looked only about one-quarter asleep. It had stubby hooves and a long tail with a soggy plume.

It bowed to Danny, then to Wendell, then Suki. Then it stood there.

"Err, right," said Danny. "So . . . what's your name?"

The baku shrugged.

"They don't talk much," said Suki.

"Um," said Wendell. "So . . . you'll come with us?"

The baku nodded.

"And eat the Dream Wasp?" asked Danny, who had some doubts about something as small and cute and weird as the baku being any use against something as big and scary-sounding as the Dream Wasp.

It considered this. It shrugged again. Then it leaned forward and peered deep into Wendell's eyes.

"What's it doing?" asked the iguana worriedly. "I don't know what it's doing!"

The baku reached out and patted Wendell's hand. And smiled.

"Right," said Danny. "I guess we've got a baku. Let's see what Great-Granddad has to say."

BARKING MAD

Getting the baku home was not as easy as Danny had hoped.

It wasn't that it was unfriendly or tried to run away. It was very friendly. It waved to the other baku as they left the clearing, and then took Wendell's hand and walked through the bamboo, making happy "mrrrp!" noises.

No, the problem was that the creature fell asleep *constantly.*

"I think it's narcoleptic," said Wendell, after the third time it suddenly dozed off in mid-stride.

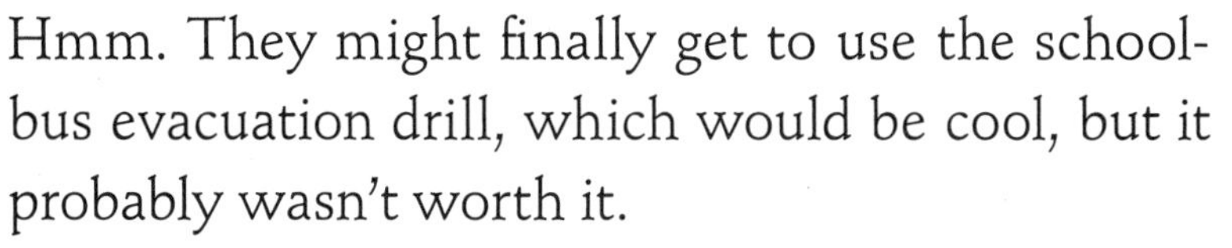

"Narco-what?"

"It's a disease," said Suki. "Or a condition or something. You fall asleep in the middle of stuff. It's a real problem if you're driving."

Danny had a vision of his school bus driver, Mr. Lyle the monitor lizard, suddenly falling asleep and driving the bus into a telephone pole. Hmm. They might finally get to use the school-bus evacuation drill, which would be cool, but it probably wasn't worth it.

"Okay, let's both take an arm . . ." he said. The baku snored.

By positioning Wendell and Danny on either side of the dream-eater, they managed to haul it back to Great-Grandfather Dragonbreath's house. The baku would fall asleep and dangle, its feet dragging, then wake up a minute later as if nothing had happened and waddle cheerfully down the path. It was very peculiar.

They reached the house and marched the baku up the stairs. It woke up, looked around happily, and was asleep by the time they reached the kitchen.

"Great-Granddaaaaaad!" yelled Danny, depositing the baku on the kitchen floor. "You didn't tell us they couldn't stay awake!"

COULDN'T MAKE CAKE? WE DON'T NEED IT FOR ITS BAKING SKILLS! GET YOUR HEAD TOGETHER, BOY!
STAY AWAKE! IT CAN'T STAY AWAKE!

"Oh, that. Yeah, they do that." The elder Dragonbreath peered down at the baku, who had leaned against the kitchen door frame and was snoring softly. "I'll get you some green tea for the trip . . ."

The baku let out a loud, warbling snore.

". . . looks like you'll need it."

Wendell had previously thought that it was hard to fall asleep with Danny watching.

He had realized now that however hard it is to fall asleep when a small dragon is staring at you, it is much, much worse when there is a small dragon, an elderly and somewhat deaf dragon, a cute salamander that is absolutely positively not your girlfriend, nope, nuh-uh, no way, and a magical creature that looks something like a tapir.

"Right," said Danny. "So Wendell falls asleep, and then Great-Granddad opens a door into the dreamworld, and Suki and I and the baku go through it to try to get to the Dream Wasp, which may or may not involve a terrible nightmarish journey through the dark horrors of Wendell's subconscious."

"There is a chance you'll go barking mad," said Great-Grandfather Dragonbreath. "With the gibbering and the foaming at the mouth. Did I mention that? I should probably mention that."

Danny waved this off as unimportant. "That doesn't matter! I have to save Wendell! It's Wendell!"

"So now we just have to wait for Wendell to fall asleep. Again," said Danny.

"Right," said the elder Dragonbreath.

"Right," said Suki.

"This is really hard with all of you watching me," said the iguana.

They'd made him up a very nice little bed on

the kitchen floor. The pillow was soft and the blankets were warm and the baku had immediately fallen asleep on his feet.

This did nothing to negate the fact that they were all staring at him.

"Now, there's a few things to remember," said Great-Grandfather Dragonbreath. "First of all, dreams can hurt you. Don't think for a moment that they can't."

"Ooo! Ooo!" Danny bounced. "Is this like the movies where they go into a computer game and it's like real and if they die in there, they die for real?"

"Corn-dog widdle!" roared Great-Grandfather Dragonbreath.

"Nobody really dies in dreams."

"People die in dreams all the time!" said Danny. "It's in all the movies!"

"Hollywood nonsense! You can die in your sleep of all sorts of things, but dreaming isn't one of them, unless your heart's so bad that you'll keel over if somebody looks at you sideways." He snorted smoke. "No, you'll be fine. It just might hurt a lot. So don't jump off any cliffs unless you absolutely have to."

"I can't imagine jumping off a cliff if I didn't absolutely have to," muttered Suki.

"I can!" said Danny.

"Second, don't get lost. Follow the buzzing and the Wasp signs. It'll leave signs of its existence around—just keep following those until you find the Wasp."

"Got it," said Suki, who was taking notes.

"Lastly, the Dream Wasp is a nasty customer. If it's already laid eggs, you'll have to deal with those. Don't let it grab your head, or it'll try to suck your dreams out. You don't want that."

"I'll burn it up if it tries!" said Danny confidently. His fire breathing had gotten a lot better. He could almost do it on command now, although he hadn't figured out how to do it without burning his tongue.

"No breathing fire," said Great-Grandfather Dragonbreath.

"Aww . . ."

"You could fry Wanda's brain with that! You're

inside his dreams, remember? A careless blast of fire, and you could fry some part of what makes him *him!* He could wake up mean or stupid or really interested in professional wrestling."

"Professional wrestling is cool," said Danny, injured.

"Is *Wanda* interested in it?"

"Well . . ." Danny had to admit that the iguana wasn't. He kept pointing out that it was all fake and what kind of sport left stacks of folding chairs just lying around the ring to break over people's heads?

"Exactly." Great-Grandfather Dragonbreath waved a claw at him. "You have to be careful in there. You can defend yourselves, but no collateral damage."

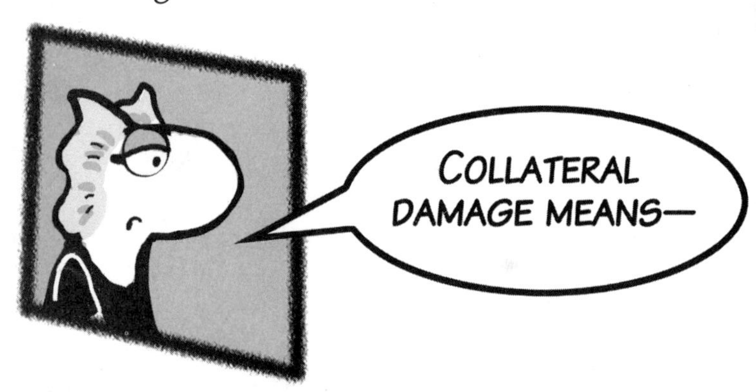

*Anything you accidentally break while trying to do something else entirely—for example, accidentally shooting an arrow through the window of a police car into the upholstery while trying to knock down a pair of underwear that you were using as a kite and which got lodged in some power lines—is collateral damage.

“Right!” said Great-Grandfather Dragonbreath. “If that’s settled, it’s time to go!”

“What?” Suki looked up. “Shouldn’t we meditate or prepare or—”

“You should have meditated before we left,” said Great-Grandfather, pointing. “No time now.”

A second snore had joined the baku’s. Wendell was fast asleep.

THE ULTIMATE MIDNIGHT SNACK

"So, about this door . . ." said Danny. He was really interested in this part. Portals to the dream-world! How cool was that? What if you could take one and get into the dreams where you could fly? "Is it a dark and mystical ritual? Do we need lots of potions and candles and stuff?"

"Do we have to center our minds and clear our consciousness?" asked Suki eagerly.

"Well, if you want to," said Great-Grandfather Dragonbreath. He stood in front of the refrigerator and fiddled with the ice maker. "Cubes . . . extra ice . . . coldest setting . . . got it!"

He opened the refrigerator door.

TA-DAH!

THE DOOR TO THE DREAMWORLD IS IN YOUR FRIDGE?

VERY USEFUL WHEN I WAKE UP IN THE MIDDLE OF THE NIGHT AND WANT A SNACK.

"Well, don't just stand there," said Great-Grandfather Dragonbreath. He made shooing motions with his hands. "Go on, go save Wanda's sanity. Poor boy needs all the help he can get. Imagine naming a boy Wanda . . ."

They got the baku on its feet. It yawned and stretched and accepted the mug of green tea from Danny's great-grandfather. The smell coming out of the mug was somewhere between tea and really angry alfalfa. Danny wondered what it could possibly taste like and then decided he didn't really want to know. The baku drank it down in three and a half gulps and sighed happily.

On the kitchen floor, Wendell mumbled in his sleep.

"Right!" said Danny. "Let's get moving!" He glanced back to make sure that Suki and the baku were following, and stepped bravely toward the portal in the fridge.

It was purple and swirly and looked like a special effect from a movie. Danny was thrilled. Here was magic that looked like magic was supposed to look!

"Don't do anything stupid," said Great-Grandfather Dragonbreath cheerfully. "Suki, try to keep track of him. And be nice to the baku. They're good luck."

Danny nodded, lifted his foot, and stepped through the portal into the dreamworld.

INSIDE THE BRAIN

The dreamworld, as it turned out, looked an awful lot like Wendell's bedroom.

There was the bed and the window and the painfully neat bookcase and Mr. Fins in his bowl and the poster of . . .

"Hang on," said Danny out loud. "That's not right."

Above Wendell's bookcase hung a poster of Super Skink. And indeed, a poster of Super Skink had hung there until two months ago, when there had been a minor mishap with a bottle-rocket-propelled balsa-wood helicopter, and the resulting

smoking crater had been in the middle of Super Skink's chest.

"What is it?" asked Suki, holding the baku's hand. "Is something wrong?" She looked around. "Is this Wendell's room?"

"I think it's a dream about his room," said Danny. "It doesn't quite look like this anymore."

"Oh." Suki considered this. "Well, that makes sense. You know, you have those dreams about your house, but it's not quite your house, and your bedroom is grafted onto the school or your grandmother's house or whatever . . ."

Danny nodded. "Right. So now we have to follow the Wasp signs. . . ."

They went over the room carefully, but there was nothing in it that looked like a trail a Wasp would leave. Danny couldn't hear any buzzing.

SKINK
SINGLE CELL

He opened the door to check the rest of the house.
It wasn't there.
"What is it?" asked Suki, peering over his shoulder.
"Doors," said Danny. "A whole lot of doors . . ."
The baku yawned and leaned against the door

frame. Danny stepped cautiously out into the hall and looked in both directions.

Nothing. Just doors, and a rather ratty carpet that looked like Wendell's brain had bought it from a motel. He couldn't even see the ends of the hallway.

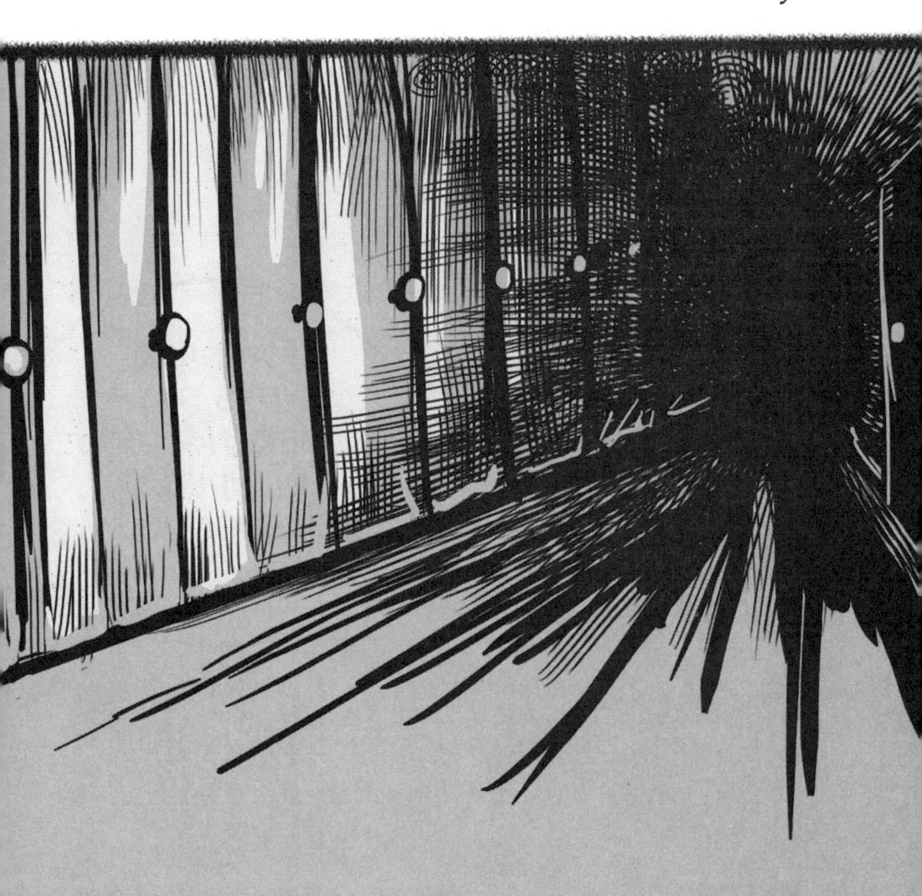

There was also a decided lack of signs saying "This Way to the Dream Wasp's Lair."

Suki tried the door opposite them and said, "It's locked."

They went down the hall, rattling each door, but all of them were locked.

The baku wandered after them, rubbing its eyes. Danny was just about to start on the seventeenth door when there was a loud thud at the other end of the hallway.

He and Suki spun around. The distant end of the hallway had gone dark.

There was another, louder thud, then another, and then the whole hallway was pounding as if someone at the end was using a jackhammer.

The darkness was coming closer, as if somebody was turning out the lights, one at a time, in sequence.

"I don't like this," said Suki.

"Yeah," said Danny. "This is not cool." He'd been in creepy hallways with bad doors before, but at least the haunted house had been *traditional.* You knew what to expect.

Something roared. The pounding was definitely closer.

"Yeah . . ." said Danny. "Yeah, I'm gonna say that we should probably run now."

Suki grabbed the baku's arm and tore off down the hall. Danny followed, grabbing the occasional door handle. They continued to be locked.

The roaring came again, and this time Danny could make out words in it.

"DO YOU WANT SOME BREWER'S YEAST!?"

It took a moment for that to sink in, and then Danny started running even faster, and actually passed Suki and the baku.

Lovely. Danny had always known that Wendell had issues with his mother—Wendell's mother lived on her issues the way that Danny's mom lived on coffee—but he'd never given it much thought. Sure, he'd once overheard his father saying something about how you'd be able to wallpaper a battleship with Wendell's therapy bills someday, but his dad refused to explain and told him never to repeat it. (He had, immediately, to Wendell, who had sighed heavily, but hadn't argued.)

Never in a million years, however, had he expected the iguana's mommy issues to try and kill him.

Thud! Thud! Thud!

"We can't keep this up!" shouted Suki. "We have to get out of this hall!"

"Grrrrp!" agreed the baku.

"The doors are locked!" said Danny, rattling another one as he passed.

"They can't all be locked!"

"Why not?"

The baku was running with its ears flat and its mane streaming. It didn't look sleepy at all now.

There was another roar, but Danny couldn't make out most of it—something about kelp, maybe—and when he risked a glance over his shoulder, the darkness was closing in.

Then he saw it.

There was a door on their left, but unlike all the others, it had something on it.

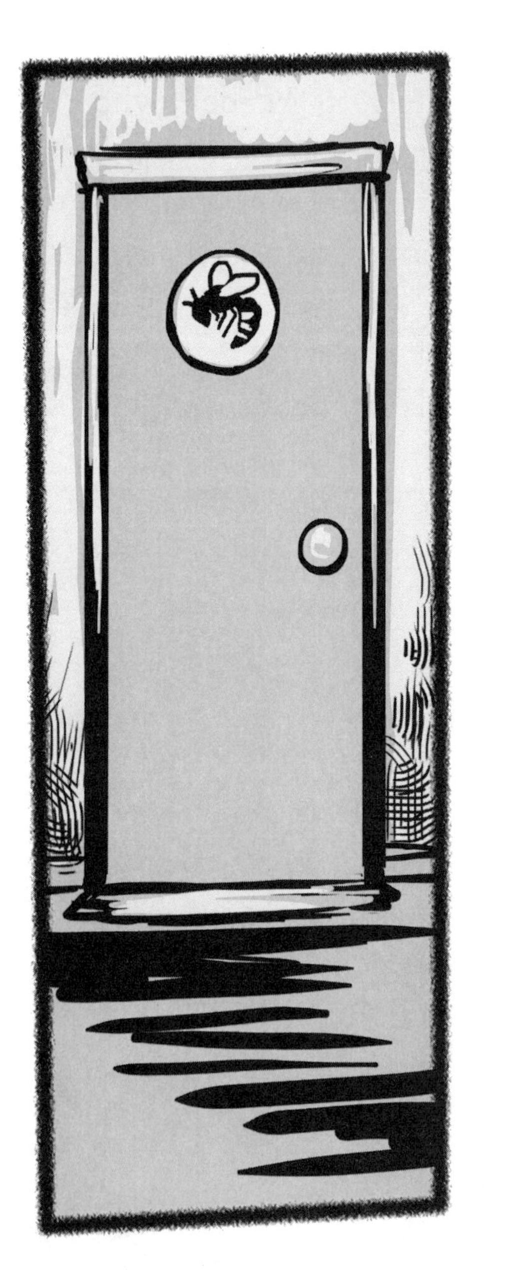

THE WASP SIGN!
IS IT UNLOCKED?

Danny skidded to a halt in front of it and grabbed the knob in both hands. The darkness was practically at their heels now, and the pounding sounded like bombs going off.

The knob turned. Danny wrenched the door open and Suki and the baku jumped inside. He leaped after them, slamming the door just as the wave of darkness crashed against it and trapped them inside.

HEALTH FOOD HORRORS

It was dark inside the room.

"I'm touching something sticky," said Suki grimly. "It feels like old gym mats. But sticky."

"Old gym mats *are* sticky," said Danny.

"Maybe at *your* school."

Danny had a sneaking suspicion that gym mats were sticky the world over, but there were more important matters at stake. The surface he was touching felt weird. It was firm but yielding, almost rubbery, but it wasn't smooth. It had a kind of rough, grainy texture, and there were deep square divots in it. The bottom of the divots was really sticky.

Danny was starting to get an idea.

Almost immediately, something began to glow.

"What's that?" asked Suki.

"I think it's the baku!" said Danny. "His tail glows! That's so cool!"

It was indeed the baku. The plume on the end of its tail was glowing as brightly as a lantern.

"Thank you!" said Suki to the baku. It looked pleased with itself and smiled until its eyes squinched up.

Danny turned his attention back to their surroundings, and realized that he'd been right.

"Those aren't gym mats," said Suki.

"Nope," said Danny. "They're . . . giant bran waffles."

It was true. They stood in an enormous cavern, the walls lost in shadow, and in front of them was a mountain of bran waffles the size of gym mats. Wendell's mom's trademark low-fat syrup glittered down the sides and congealed in the hollows near the floor.

"Well," said Danny. "That's . . . something." He wished Wendell were here. Wendell would have something clever and snarky to say, and then Danny could give him a hard time about having gigantic waffle dreams.

"I don't want to alarm you," said Suki, in a tone that indicated she was somewhat alarmed, "but the door's gone."

Danny looked. The wall was a smooth expanse of gray stone with no door anywhere.

"Hmm. Well, we didn't want to go back there anyway."

"There's some different stuff over there," said Suki, pointing. The baku moved its tail, throwing wild shadows across the room.

The light fell on slices of pickled beets the size of truck tires and Brussels sprouts as large as boulders.

"It looks like all that health food is getting to him," said Danny.

"Really? I would *never* have guessed . . ."

Danny had forgotten that Suki could be really sarcastic when she put her mind to it.

"Do you see anything that looks like a wasp?" asked Danny.

"No . . ."

"I guess we should start walking, then." Danny took a deep breath and prepared to ascend Mt. Waffle.

The syrup made it an unpleasant climb, but there were plenty of handholds.

When they reached the top, there was still nothing obviously wasp-like. Quivering towers of tofu loomed out of the darkness around them.

"I like tofu," said Suki. "You just have to cook it right."

"Urggh," said Danny. "Let's not stop for a snack."

They walked down the far side of the waffle mountain. There was a small bubbling lake of yogurt, with a beach made out of some kind of wet grainy stuff.

"Tabouli," said Suki. "It's an acquired taste. I've never wanted to acquire it."

The baku grabbed Danny's arm and pointed.

On the far side of the tabouli beach, past a log-jam of giant bean sprouts, rose a dripping honeycomb.

"Wasp sign!" said Danny. "Good job!"

"Do wasps make honey? I thought bees made honey."

The baku shrugged. "Mrrp?"

"I think some wasps make honey." Danny wished Wendell were here again—he'd definitely know. "Can't hurt to check it out."

The honeycomb was much stickier than the syrup. Golden honey oozed out of it and glittered on the ground.

"I don't know why he'd be having nightmares about this," said Danny. "This looks awesome!"

"Maybe dreams don't work like that," said Suki. "I mean, for all we know, this is like . . . like the prop department in a theater. Whenever

there's a dream about food, they pull it out of here. So it's not that he's having specific dreams about this stuff, this is just where all the food dreams end up."

"Wow." Danny had to think about that one. "So, like . . . there could be all kinds of different storerooms! You could keep scenery in one and costumes and pirate ships and cars—"

"Boxes for those dreams where you're trying to pack—" said Suki.

"—apartments for the monsters to live in—"

They walked around the honeycomb. On the far side, there was a small door, and in the middle was the wasp symbol from the first door.

"Jackpot!" said Danny. He reached for the knob and took a last look around the strange health-food landscape. "Say, Suki . . ."

"Yes?"

"Assuming you're right about there being different places dream stuff is stored . . ."

"Yes?"

"I wonder if we can find where they keep all the weapons and stuff . . ."

THE NERD-BRARY

The wasp door led into a . . . well, Danny supposed you'd call it a library. Maybe.

Calling this building a library was kind of like calling the Ultimate Mecha-Fighter Newt 9000 with Kung-Fu Grip and Bullet Launching Action a doll. You could make a case, but you'd really be missing the point.

"Whoa," said Danny.

"It's like a cathedral," said Suki.

The baku hummed happily and doused the light in its tail.

This was a temple to books. There were bookcases in every direction, as far as the eye could see. Sunbeams streamed between the shelves and motes of dust danced in them.

Suki took down a book near them and opened it up. *"The vampire squid,"* she read, *"despite its fearsome appearance, is a shy creature that shoots phosphorescent mucus to escape predators."*

It was a testimony to Suki's academic skills that she could say "phosphorescent" without stumbling over it. Danny would have required four or five tries and possibly a running start.

YOU MEAN THAT EVERYTHING HE KNOWS IS IN HERE?

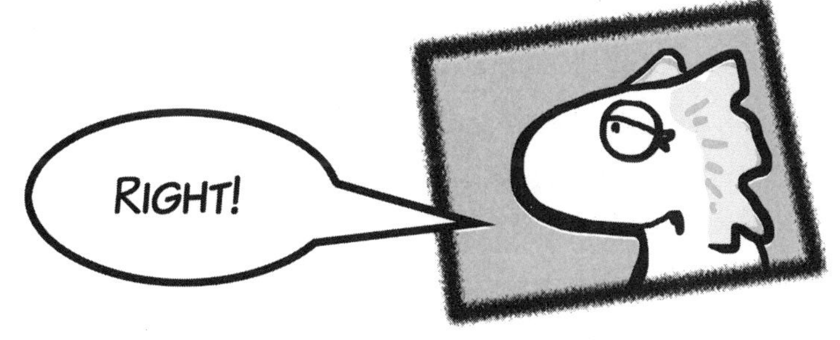
RIGHT!

OH, MAN . . . THIS PLACE IS GONNA BE *HUGE* . . .

It was. When they emerged into the main body of the library, there were staircases every which way, leading up to other floors and down into the depths. Walkways crisscrossed over their heads. Even the pillars holding up the ceiling seemed to be made of books.

Small, hooded figures walked between the bookcases. They didn't look threatening. When one walked by, it lifted its hood, revealing a pale reptile face, and whispered "Shhhhh. . . ." before walking on.

"How are we going to find a wasp door in this?" whispered Danny, discouraged. The dragon was willing to defy death for Wendell, fight off hordes of savage enemies, navigate landscapes of health food and horror . . . but going to the library was something else. You could tell this wasn't the sort of library that had kids' books and a comic book section. This reminded him of the law library that his mother sometimes went to. There was nothing fun going on there. You checked fun at the door.

Suki tugged on the frill of gills around her head. "Hmm. You know . . . this is *Wendell* we're talking about. I think I have an idea."

The salamander strode confidently into the center of the library, up to a hooded librarian. "Excuse me," she said. "Can you tell me where the card catalog is?"

The librarian turned and slowly pushed back its hood. It was very pale and had a black frill. Its eyes were dark and seemed to swim with stars.

"We're looking for a book on wasps," said Suki.

THANK YOU!

The card catalog was the size of an eighteen-wheeler. They had to trudge around it to get to the *W*'s, and then Suki needed a footstool to be able to reach it.

"You know, they have all this on computers now," said Danny, leaning against the *V*'s.

"I know that and you know that . . ." said Suki, flipping cards. "Wendell says card catalogs don't

crash. He's got strong opinions on library organization and believes that you should always leave a hard-copy backup."

"Seriously?" said Danny. "Is this the sort of thing you talk about in your love letters?"

"They're not love letters. And you should hear him talk about the Dewey Decimal System."

"I have," said Danny. "Believe me."

"W . . . W . . . War . . . Wards . . .Warps . . . Washing machines . . . Washington . . . Aha! Wasps!"

She scribbled the shelf numbers on a scrap of paper and scrambled down.

There were signposts on the pillars, with arrows. Suki consulted one, then strode off into the depths of the library. Danny followed, stopping to wake up the baku along the way.

They reached a large section of bookcases that ran clear to the ceiling. They were set so close together that the kids could only walk single file between them.

Suki ran her finger over a row of bindings.

"Wasps . . . let's see . . . *The Time I Stepped on a Bee and It Stung Me—*"

"I remember that," said Danny.

"His memories are all jumbled up in here with facts," Suki complained. "It's not as organized as it could be. *Facts About Honey* is next to *The Time We Stayed Up Late and Watched* Revenge of the Killer Bees from Jupiter."

Danny also remembered that, and was about to offer his review—the killer bees had been the best actors in the movie—when he heard somebody shouting.

It was such a shocking sound in the library that both Suki and the baku jumped, and even Danny might have twitched a little.

"Keep looking," said Danny. "I'll go check."

He hurried to the end of the bookcase and peered out.

There was a monster in the library.

EMBARRASSING BRAIN BOOKS

It was tall and shaggy and had horns. It glared grimly down at a horde of tiny librarians, who were shushing it for all they were worth.

"Out of my way!" it roared. "There are intruders in the dreamlands! We have story problems for them!"

"SHHHHHH!" whispered the librarians.

"I'll not be shushed, ye pestilent book-botherers! Stand aside!"

"SHHHHHH!" hissed the librarians, even louder.

Danny hunched down, trying to hide behind a few large books sticking out from the shelves. A title caught his eye—*Reasons Suki Is Awesome.*

"Oh, good grief," muttered Danny.

The volume next to it was twice as thick and titled *Reasons That I Will Die of Shame if Suki Ever Finds Out I Like Her.*

Occasionally Danny wondered how Wendell managed to keep it together long enough to function at all.

A second monster stomped into the library. It was wide and hairy and had enormous hooves that clopped on the stone floor. "They're in here somewhere!" it yelled.

"I know!" shouted the first monster.

A third monster joined them. This one looked like a buffalo carrying a battle-ax. "Any luck?" it yelled.

Danny thought the librarians were going to faint, but they were made of sterner stuff. Two of

them crouched down and lifted a third on their shoulders. It braced its feet, cupped its hands to its mouth, and shouted:

"Quiet in the library, please!"

Danny didn't stick around to see how the monsters reacted. He ran back down the line of shelves. "Suki! There are monsters in the library! I think we need to go, now!" (He decided not to mention the books.)

"I can't find it!" said Suki. "I thought there would be a book here that could show us, or maybe one that would activate a secret door—you know, like in the movies! But I can't find anything useful!"

Danny looked around wildly. He could hear the monsters clomping around, less than fifty feet away. How long would the librarians be able to hold them?

"Get these runts out of my way!" bellowed one of the monsters. "The dreamlands must be protected from intruders!"

"We will crush their bones and then give them pop quizzes!" cried the monster beside it.

The baku jumped frantically up and down and pointed.

Danny and Suki followed its pointing finger up . . . and up . . .

Near the ceiling, in the middle of the row of books, was one marked with the wasp sign.

"Oh, crud," said Suki. "One of us is going to have to climb."

The *clomp-clomp-clomp* of the monsters' hooves was getting closer.

"I'll do it." Danny pushed up his sleeves. "It's a big bookcase. It's practically like a ladder."

"Right," said Suki. "We'll . . . um . . . guard your back."

The baku rolled its eyes.

The first few shelves were easy. Then Danny ran into a set of encyclopedias that came right over the edge of the shelf and didn't leave him any handholds. He had to inch sideways to the

next bookcase and go up that one instead until he passed the treacherous tomes.

The clomping hooves came nearer and nearer . . . and stopped.

"They're over here, boss!" yelled the buffalo-shaped monster.

Danny lunged up the bookcase, his heart pounding. His fingers closed over a copy of *That Time the Grasshopper Jumped in My Eye When I Was Three* and sent it spinning to the ground.

The monsters were too big to fit in the narrow lane between the bookcases. One of them tried and got its shoulders stuck. The buffalo lowered its head and pawed at the ground.

"Tear the bookcase apart!" ordered the one in charge.

The buffalo monster charged at a bookcase. Books exploded in a whirl of pages. The shock went down the line of bookcases and Danny's perch shook violently. One of his feet slipped. He grabbed at *The Time I Stepped on a Bee and Had to Go to the Emergency Room* for support.

"Danny!" yelled Suki. And then: "Stop that, you stupid monster! You can't do that to books!"

The monster did not seem to agree. It hit the bookcase again, and there was a groan as the wood started to give way. Shelves splintered.

The buffalo looked vaguely confused. Apparently people did not yell at it often.

Danny got both his feet under him again and practically jumped the rest of the way up the bookcase. He could see the wasp-sign book clearly now. It was stuck between *Theory of Colony Collapse Syndrome* and *Macro Insect Photography Through the Ages.*

GOT IT!
HURRY!

MEMORY
Z

The monster with the battle-ax swung and hit the weakened bookcase. It collapsed slowly. Books slid off in a waterfall of paper.

"Catch!" yelled Danny, and dropped the wasp book.

Suki caught it and flipped it open. Danny turned back to the bookcase and began climbing down as fast as he could. Every blow of the battle-ax shook him until his teeth rattled.

"Are there directions?" he shouted. "What do we do?"

"Actually . . ." said Suki, sounding very strange, "it's . . . stairs."

"What?"

The bookcases shook again. Danny looked over, saw the monsters less than a dozen feet away, and decided that climbing was overrated when falling was so much faster. He pushed off from the shelves and jumped.

He landed on the baku. It snorted in its sleep, but didn't wake up.

Suki looked up at him. Her face was alight with amazement. “Look at it!” she said, and held the book out to him.

There were no words. Instead, there was a square cut out in the middle of the book, which led to a staircase. Leading down.

“It’s like three inches thick,” said Suki. “I’m holding the bottom. But look—you can stick your hand in—they’re real stairs! It goes somewhere else, through the book!”

The next bookcase collapsed. A blizzard of pages fell around them.

"It's impossible!" said Suki. "It's unnatural! It's *weird*!"

"Good enough for me!" said Danny. He grabbed the baku's arm, shook it awake, and jumped into the book feet-first.

MONSTER BULLY

They were real stairs. They were stone and they went down quite a long way.

They were also extremely slippery, and Danny's leap caused him to skid down two steps and nearly land on his tail, but he caught himself in time. The baku yawned and padded along behind him, and Suki jumped in afterward.

"I wish we could close the book behind us," she said. "What if the monsters follow us?"

"Do you think they can fit?" It had been a big book, but not that big.

"Who knows?"

There was a clopping, straining sound. Somebody had managed to fit a leg into the book. A giant hoof scrabbled for purchase on the stairs.

"Or, y'know, we could run," said Suki.

That was one of the things Danny liked about Suki. She was always practical about things like this.

They hurried down the steps as quickly as they could. They couldn't quite run—the steps were too slick—but they jogged.

There was a second clomp. Danny glanced back and saw most of the lower half of a monster at the top of the stairs. It seemed to have a hard time getting its shoulders through.

"You know," said Suki as they jogged, "my mom watches this show called *My Dream Wedding*. It's one of her favorites."

". . . okay . . ." said Danny, wondering where this was going. "Sounds lame."

"Oh, you have no idea. It's crazy. People spend,

like, a year's salary so the bride can ride down the aisle on a white donkey or something. And they close out every week with the bride gushing about how this was just like a dream, it was all so *dreamy,* it was her dream come *true . . .*"

The baku snickered.

"Exactly," said Suki, nodding to the little creature. "The next time I see one of those, I'm gonna say 'What, your wedding was like running down a staircase inside a book while monsters chase you, looking for a giant wasp?'"

The monster had gotten one arm into the book and was trying to haul the rest of itself through the hole. Grunting and swearing echoed down the stone steps after them.

There was something oddly familiar about the arm.

"I am getting a little worried that this staircase has been going on for a long time and we don't seem to be getting anywhere," said Suki, before Danny could place it.

They reached a broad landing. The stairs turned sharply to the right and continued on, apparently forever.

"GOT IT!" roared the monster at the top of the stairs. Danny couldn't see it anymore, but the rattle of hooves on stone sounded like gunfire in the tight stairwell.

"This would be an awesome time for a wasp door," said Danny, to no one in particular.

"Agreed," said Suki. The baku nodded.

A wasp door did not materialize. The stairs cut sharply to the left. The baku slipped on a step and bounced down nearly a dozen steps.

NO!
Z...

"He fell asleep in *mid-fall?*" asked Suki in disbelief.

"Guess the green tea's wearing off."

They shook the baku awake. It didn't seem to have been bruised at all. It rolled to its feet, mrrping cheerfully, and resumed jogging down the stairs.

"Intruders!" roared the monster behind them. "I hear you! You violate the sanctity of the dreamlands! *I want your lunch money!*"

Danny remembered where he'd seen an arm like that before.

He leaned back at the next landing and his worst fears were confirmed. The monster did have hooves and horns, and it was very tall . . . and it also looked a lot like the school bully, Big Eddy.

Suki and Danny exchanged glances and put on an extra burst of speed. The monster sounded much closer than was comfortable.

"It's Big Eddy, isn't it?" asked Suki.

“Wendell’s pretty scared of him,” said Danny. “I guess it’s not surprising that he’s a monster in Wendell’s brain . . .”

“THERE WILL BE QUIZZES!” screamed the Big Eddy bison-thing.

“We’re here to help!” yelled Danny over his shoulder. “We’re Wendell’s frien—”

And then he had to stop and dive for Suki’s tail, because the stairs had ended abruptly.

At the top of a cliff.

INTO THE ABYSS

It was a very tall cliff. Danny couldn't see the bottom of it. Clouds drifted by, shockingly white on a gloomy gray sky.

"I hate cliffs," said Suki, dangling over the abyss. "Really. Ever since that thing with the ninjas and the volcano, I have not been a fan."

Danny managed to haul the salamander girl up onto the ledge at the end of the stairs. She knelt on the stone and gripped it tightly with the squishy pads of her fingers.

"Intruders!" yelled the Big Eddy monster from behind them. The clomp of hooves sounded like jackhammers and thunder.

"There's nowhere else to go," said Danny grimly, looking to either side. "I think we'll have to jump."

JUMP? IT'S LIKE A MILLION FEET DOWN!

I KNOW! ISN'T IT AWESOME? I SAW A SHOW ON CLIFF-DIVING A FEW WEEKS AGO AND I'VE BEEN DYING TO TRY IT!

FALLING TO OUR DEATHS IS NOT AWESOME!

"Remember? It's all a dream! Great-Granddad said!"

"He also said not to jump off any cliffs!"

"Not unless we absolutely have to," agreed Danny. He pointed up the stairs. "And I'm pretty sure we absolutely have to!"

The monster burst into view. Big Eddy's face was not improved by adding horns and a shaggy mane. It looked very upset.

"Outsiders in the dreamlands!" it roared. It lowered its head and charged down the remaining stairs.

Suki looked at Danny, looked at the monster, looked behind her, said to no one in particular, "Look, Wendell's cute, but I'm not sure if he's worth all this."

Danny grabbed the baku and hurried to the cliff edge. "C'mon! Let's go!"

"I can't do it! It's a cliff!" She looked wildly between the approaching monster and the clouds below. "You go! I'll—I'll figure something out—"

"Suki!"

The monster grabbed the edges of the door frame and skidded to a halt. Danny could hear it breathing in great whuffling gasps as it stared at them.

"We're trying to help!" said Suki.

The Big Eddy monster took a threatening step forward.

The baku grabbed Suki's tail and began tugging her toward the cliff, making worried noises.

"Suki . . ." said Danny.

The salamander folded her arms tightly around her chest. "I really don't like cliffs," she said grimly. "I'm scared, okay?"

Inspiration struck Danny like lightning.

The monster took another step forward, clenching its fists, but Danny didn't get time to appreciate this, because Suki had just punched him in the shoulder. For a girl, she had a pretty impressive punch.

She whirled around and threw herself into empty space. The baku, who was still clinging to her tail, let out a whoop and went over as well.

A monster-sized fist was coming at Danny's head. Danny ducked under it, wished briefly that he was allowed to breathe fire—he'd always wanted to set Big Eddy on fire, but grown-ups frowned on that sort of thing—gave the creature a kick in the shins instead, and flung himself after Suki and into the abyss.

THINGS GET STRANGE

Falling off the cliff was surprisingly peaceful.

Sure, Danny's stomach appeared to have been left somewhere back with the monster, but the fall apparently went on forever. He could even control which way he was falling by tilting his shoulders and using his tail as a rudder. It was kind of like swimming in the air.

He could see Suki and the baku ahead of him. There was a cloud coming up—they vanished into it—and then it was all around him, cold and wet and damp—and then they were through. There hadn't been very much to it at all.

"So that's what a cloud feels like!" shouted Danny. "I thought it'd be more . . . I dunno . . . cottony!"

"I'm not talking to you!" Suki yelled back.

Danny rolled his eyes. Would she rather have gotten stomped by a monster from Wendell's nightmares?

Still, at least she'd actually jumped. If it had been Wendell himself, Danny would have had to throw him off the cliff.

Presumably they'd hit the bottom at some point, but that seemed like a long ways away. They'd been falling for several minutes now. Apparently cliffs were a lot taller in people's heads. The baku had fallen asleep again.

Another cloud went past them. Danny found that by tucking his arms in tight against his body, he could fall faster. He zipped downward until he was nearly even with Suki and the baku.

THIS IS SO COOL!
SHUT UP.

The wasp-shaped cloud loomed under them. It was off to one side, and they had to angle themselves to fall toward it. Danny started to worry that they might miss it completely, but after a minute he realized that the cloud was much bigger than he thought. It was the size of a mountain at least.

"Do you hear that?" yelled Suki, who had apparently forgotten that she wasn't talking to him.

"Yeah!"

Danny could hear it just fine.

It was the same whole-hive-of-angry-wasps buzzing he'd heard in Wendell's bedroom.

It was coming from the cloud.

BZZZzzzzZZZzzzzZZZZ

"That's a really bad sound!" said Suki.

"I told you it was!"

It got louder as they fell toward the cloud. It seemed to crawl in Danny's ears and around his rib cage and vibrate inside his bones. His teeth were buzzing in his jaw as if a dentist were drilling on them.

The baku had woken up and was clutching its head.

"We must be close!" yelled Danny.

"Assuming we don't just fall right through the cloud!"

"We're about to find out!"

WE'RE HEADED FOR THE THORAX!
I THOUGHT THORAX WAS A HEAVY METAL BAND!

Suki started to explain to him about wasp anatomy and its lack of relation to popular music, shouting to make herself heard over the buzzing, but about then they fell into the giant wasp cloud and things started to get a little strange.

RIDING THE NIGHT MARE

Danny realized that he wasn't falling anymore.

It wasn't as if he'd landed on something. There wasn't a shock of impact. He'd been falling through a cold white expanse, with that horrible buzzing roaring in his ears, and then he just wasn't falling anymore.

Actually, he seemed to be sitting on something.

Something moving.

Something alive.

Something with bones that were poking him in uncomfortable places. It wasn't as bad as riding a jackalope last summer had been, but it was still awfully bony.

Was he riding a horse? He couldn't see his hand in front of his face. All he could see was the white fog of the cloud.

The creature under him made a sound like no horse had ever made—a shriek like tearing metal that cut through the buzzing—and then the cloud fell away—or they broke out of it—and—

"Oh, *dude,*" said Danny.

He was riding a Night Mare.

Its back was bony and slicked with sweat. He could feel its ribs sticking out against his legs. He grabbed for the mare's whipping mane and held on. The creature was running through the clouds, which had pulled back into a soggy white tunnel. Its hooves sunk into the cloud like mud and pulled out again with soft sucking sounds. Danny twisted his head to look behind him and saw that they were leaving a trail of glowing hoofprints.

He also saw Suki, which was an enormous relief. She was clinging grimly to the back of a second Night Mare.

"Where are they taking us?" she called. Her mount let out another screaming metal whinny and seemed to snicker.

"I don't know!" yelled Danny. "Where's the baku?" If they'd lost the dream-eater, the whole trip was useless . . . although arguably, any trip where he got to ride an actual Night Mare had a lot to recommend it. Still, he didn't want Wendell to go insane. That would be bad. And someone was bound to notice eventually.

Suki pointed over his shoulder.

Danny turned back and saw the baku.

The little creature was riding the biggest Night Mare of all, and for once it didn't look sleepy. It clung to the mare's mane and slapped the horse's bony flank with its tail.

"Whoa," said Danny.

The tunnel split into two branches, and the

baku's Night Mare tried to veer into the left-hand one. The baku yanked its mane around and pointed it toward the right-hand tunnel.

Danny wasn't sure if he was going to be able to haul his own steed's head around—riding without a saddle or bridle was not a lot of fun, particularly if you were a boy and the horse had a

spine that appeared to be made out of coat hangers—but his Night Mare clung close to the heels of the first one. When he looked back, Suki was still following.

"I think the baku's leading them!" he shouted.

Suki nodded. "And the buzzing's getting louder!"

Twice more the tunnel split, and twice more the baku drove the lead Night Mare into the tunnel of the baku's choosing. Both times the buzzing got louder.

Danny couldn't hear anything anymore. If Suki yelled to him, he missed it.

The Night Mares clearly didn't like the buzzing at all, but they were herd animals and were intent on following their leader. Danny's steed had its ears flat back against its skull and kept shaking its head.

Danny knew just how it felt.

The tunnel split into three passages. Two led left and right, deeper into the white cloud, but the center one was dark and narrow. It looked like a mouth. The buzzing that came out of it was so loud that Danny thought he'd be rattled right off the mare's back.

The baku leaned low over the lead Night Mare's neck. The dream horse tried to veer left, then right—actually bucked a few times—but the baku held tight. With a another metallic scream, it plunged into the dark tunnel.

Danny flung himself as low on the Night Mare's back as he could. The ceiling was so low that he could have put up a hand and touched it, and it didn't look like a cloud anymore. For a moment, the glowing hoofprints were the only source of light in the darkness.

Then the room opened up. A flare of green-gold light nearly blinded them. All three Night Mares let out a metallic scream, like a car being torn apart, and slid to a halt.

Danny blinked away tears from the sudden light and saw the baku leap down from its mare. He didn't get a chance to follow, because his own steed took that opportunity to buck violently and throw him off onto the ground. Danny let out a yelp, rolled, and came to rest on . . . something.

It wasn't stone. It wasn't cloud. It wasn't even bran waffle.

It felt like wax.

Another yelp and a thud told him that Suki was getting the same treatment. Danny lifted his head and saw that they were in an enormous chamber. The walls were covered in honeycomb.

The baku, looking grim, was standing in front of him. Beyond the dream-eater perched a creature far more nightmarish than the Night Mares.

The buzzing stopped.

BATTLE ZONE

The Dream Wasp was the size of a house. Danny was no stranger to giant monsters—he'd met a few, and one had even been kind of friendly—but this one looked *mean.*

Its stinger was as long as a car and tapered to a wickedly sharp point. Its jaws were serrated and meshed together like a bone zipper. Its forelegs looked like steak knives, assuming that by "steak" you meant "the entire cow."

"Eeep," said Suki.

Danny was very glad she'd said it, because that meant he didn't have to.

The whole room looked like the inside of a hive. Pillars of honeycomb rose haphazardly from floor to ceiling. The three Night Mares were trying to hide behind one.

Gigantic wings fanned out behind the Dream Wasp. They were the source of the buzzing. While Danny watched, it gave them a shake, and a loud buzz ran briefly through the room.

"Look!" whispered Suki, pointing. "Eggs!"

"We've got to destroy them!" Danny whispered back. "If they hatch, Wendell will go crazy!"

"Yeah, but we can't let the baku fight *that,*" said Suki. "Look at it! It's huge!"

Danny gulped. The salamander was right. The baku looked *tiny.* Asking it to eat a dream the size of the Dream Wasp would be like Danny trying to eat a whale. There was just no way.

The baku patted both of their hands, smiled, and turned away. Then it began to waddle toward the Dream Wasp.

"Baku—" said Danny desperately. Suki put a hand to her mouth.

The Dream Wasp spoke.

"Eaterrrrrr offfff Dreamsszzzzzzzz," it buzzed, in a whining voice that made Danny's spine want to climb out of his body and go someplace less scary.

The Night Mares stamped and shivered and tried to cram themselves behind the honeycomb pillar. Danny kind of wished he could join them, but Suki would never let him hear the end of it. Also, Wendell. Best friend. Insanity. Right.

"You arrrre too ssssszzzzzmall," buzzed the Dream Wasp. "I will desszzzzztroy you."

The baku continued to waddle forward. It did not look concerned. It looked more like it had just seen a comfortable place for a nap.

"Is it just me," whispered Suki, "or is the baku getting bigger? And its tail . . . ?"

Danny squinted. For a second he wasn't sure—the size of the room and the Wasp made it hard to tell—but then the baku started growing and there was no question.

By the time the baku reached the Dream Wasp,

it wasn't little and cute anymore. Its tail was glowing like a neon sign. And it *definitely* didn't look sleepy.

"Whoa," said Danny.

"Thiszzzz dreamer iszzzzz not imporrrrtant," sizzled the Wasp. "He iszzzz only a foolisssszzzzh child. Hissszzzz madnesszzzzz will taszzzzzzte ssssszzzweet. Leavvvvvve him to me."

"Hey!" yelled Suki. "That's my boyfriend you're talking about!"

"And that's my best friend you're— Wait, really?" Danny turned to Suki. "Ha! I knew it!"

"Well, it's long-distance," muttered Suki. "I mean, it's not really *formal*. But I mean . . . um . . . Look, can we talk about this later?"

The baku grinned. Its previously stubby tusks were nearly as big as Danny.

"Sssszzzztay away!" screamed the Dream Wasp, cowering back, and the baku pounced.

The floor shook as the two collided. The Wasp slashed with its bladed forearms, but the baku's hide was thick and knobbly, and it barely seemed to notice. The dream-eater bore the monster down to the floor, crushing the giant insect under its weight, while its glowing tail whipped wildly through the air.

“Quick!” said Danny. “While it’s distracted! Squish the eggs!” He jumped into the pile. Eggs crunched under his feet.

They ranged in size from grapefruit to bowling balls, and squishing them was really disgusting.

Suki bit her lower lip and kept her eyes closed. Bits of wasp yolk splashed the bottom of her dress.

"Ninjapants!" she muttered. "This is horrible. I would rather jump off ten cliffs. Oh god, this is disgusting. . . ."

Danny was normally a fan of both gross things and wanton destruction, but he had to agree. He'd never leave rotten eggs in Big Eddy's mailbox again. There were things squishing between his toes that he didn't want to think about, particularly considering that wasps were bugs, and baby bugs were maggots or grubs or—

No, he definitely didn't want to think about it.

"Uh-oh," said Suki.

Danny shot a glance over his shoulder at the fight, and gulped.

The Dream Wasp was winning. One of its wings hung askew and it was missing a bladed leg, but it had knocked the baku down and was trying to stab the dream-eater with its stinger.

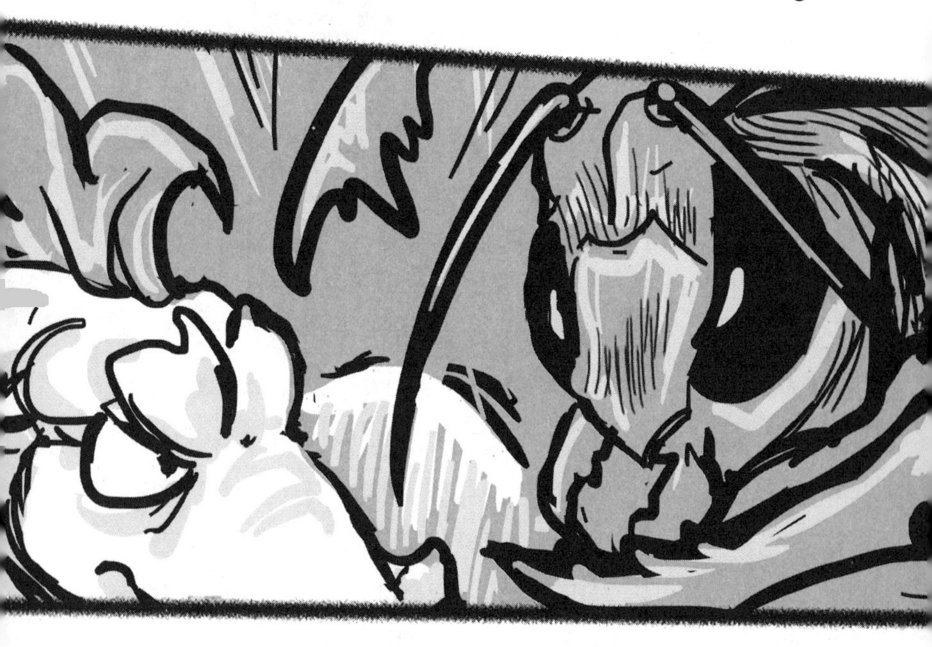

"We have to help!" Suki cried.

"I know!" Danny yelled back. What could he do?

He couldn't breathe fire! He looked around wildly for something to throw.

There was only one thing at hand.

Danny grabbed a softball-sized wasp egg, wound up, and pitched a line drive directly into the Dream Wasp's eye.

The egg splattered. The Wasp shrieked, whether in outrage or in pain, Danny couldn't tell.

Suki hurled three more eggs with the deadly accuracy that had earned her the respect of girls' softball teams in two different countries.

The baku rolled to its feet and shook itself.

The Wasp, bizarrely, ignored it, screaming, "My egggsszzz! Egg-killlerzzzzz! I will sszzting you and ssszzzting you—!"

"I think it's mad," said Danny.

"Really?" asked Suki. "Whatever gave you that idea?"

Danny saw that the creature, despite missing a leg, was pulling itself along the floor, sinking the great bladed legs deep into the honeycomb and dragging itself forward. Those terrible jaws seemed to fill Danny's vision.

The baku landed on the Wasp's back with a sickening final crunch. Suki grabbed Danny's arm and yanked him out of the way as the Dream Wasp convulsed, legs whipping. The dragon felt one whoosh an inch past his head.

He decided that he forgave Suki for not talking to him when they were falling off the cliff earlier. He might not be able to die in Wendell's dreams, but having a giant bladed wasp leg stuck in his head would not have been much fun.

The Wasp's legs moved like a wind-up toy running down. The baku's tail glowed so brightly that it was hard to look at, then let out an enormous green flash.

Danny sat up, blinking spots out of his vision.

"I think it's dead," said Suki.

"That was *amazing,*" said Danny.

THE GIRL OF WENDELL'S DREAMS

They rode the Night Mares out of the dreamlands. After watching the baku dispatch the Dream Wasp, the horses weren't inclined to argue with the little creature. "They're not *bad,*" said Suki. "They're attracted to bad dreams, but they look a lot scarier than they are." She patted hers on the neck. It whuffled.

It was a short trip. Danny didn't remember getting off the Night Mare, but a moment later he came out of the refrigerator door, tripped over a chair, and fell on the linoleum.

"Took you long enough," said Great-Grandfather Dragonbreath. "You think I can afford to leave the fridge open for hours? I'm air-conditioning the entire house this way!"

"Great-Granddad!" Danny sat up. "The baku! It was huge—it had claws—and the Wasp—"

"Well, they do that," said Great-Grandfather Dragonbreath. He reached out and helped Suki step down from the refrigerator portal, then slammed the door. "And I've been dying for a sandwich this entire time," he added, opening the door again to reveal a perfectly ordinary refrigerator.

“Is Wendell okay?” asked Suki. “We squashed the eggs! And is the baku okay? The Wasp didn’t hurt it?”

“I think the baku’s fine,” said Danny dryly. He pointed.

On the floor, curled up against Wendell’s side, the baku was fast asleep.

THE BAKU SAVED YOU, WANDA. YOU SHOULDN'T HAVE ANY MORE WASP PROBLEMS.

PLEASE TELL IT THANK YOU.

AND TELL IT THAT IT'S *AWESOME!*

"So, um," said Suki a few minutes later as they waited at the bus stop. Great-Grandfather Dragonbreath had kicked them out, saying that he needed a nap after that sandwich.

"Um," said Wendell. He stared at his feet. "I hope you guys didn't . . . err . . . see anything too weird in there. . . ."

"There was plenty of weird stuff," said Danny. "I didn't know a grasshopper jumped in your eye when you were little!"

"Unnnnggh!" Wendell shuddered. "All those little legs, and it was RIGHT THERE. . . ."

Danny snickered. He was tempted to tell Wendell about the books about Suki, but maybe not while the salamander was standing right there.

"I think that's my bus," said Suki, looking up. "Ah . . . well . . . Wendell, you know, if we can both get to Danny's great-grandfather's place, maybe we could . . . um . . ."

"We could hang out sometime," said Wendell. "Yeah. I'd like that. Um."

Danny rolled his eyes.

The bus pulled up. "Thanks for your help, Suki," said Danny. "I couldn't have done it without you. I would never have figured out the card catalog, for one thing."

"Sure," said Suki. She looked at Wendell. Wendell looked at her.

"Um," said Wendell. "You, uh. Saved me. I, uh . . . I mean . . . if you ever . . . um . . ."

She ran up the little steps into the bus. It let out of a hiss of brakes and drove away.

"I saved you *too*," said Danny.

"I'm not kissing you."

"Wendell's got a girrrrrlfriend," said Danny, delighted.

"Shut up."

"Besides," said Danny. "You know I think Suki's cool. And now you practically *have* to be her boyfriend."

"I do?"

"Sure!" Danny waved his hands. "She's been in your subconscious! She even called you her boyfriend while we were in there! Now she's . . . *the girl of your dreams!*"

Wendell groaned. "I will destroy you *twice.*"

A bus appeared in the distance. The iguana fidgeted.

After a moment, he said, "Did she really call me her boyfriend?"

Danny rolled his eyes again.

"You know," he said, after a minute, as the bus rolled closer, "we have brunch at my house every Saturday. Without bran waffles."

"Really?" asked Wendell, sounding almost as hopeful as he had about being Suki's boyfriend.

"Really," said Danny, and waited for the bus to come and pick them up and take them away to another adventure.

Zzzzz . . .
Zzz

THERE'S A THIEF AT SUNNY ACRES REPTILE HOME

And if Danny doesn't find out who—or what—has been stealing dentures and lawn ornaments, his crabby granddad will come and live with him. In. His. Room.

But even mutant thieves don't stand a chance when Danny, his nerdy friend Wendell, and their friend-who-is-a-girl Christiana are on the case.

DON'T MISS
THE CASE OF THE TOXIC MUTANTS
COMING SOON!